For Charlie and Parker —NF

Library of Congress Cataloging-in-Publication Data
Names: Feuti, Norman, author, illustrator. | Feuti, Norman. Hello, Hedgehog! ; 4.
Title: Let's go swimming! / Norm Feuti.
Description: New York : Acorn/Scholastic inc., 2021. | Series: Hello, Hedgehog! ; 4 | Summary: On a hot day, Hedgehog and his best friend, Harry, go swimming in the pond to cool off—and when Hedgehog helps his friend overcome his fear of going underwater, they find a treasure.
Identifiers: LCCN 2020030126 | ISBN 9781338677119 (paperback) | ISBN 9781338677126 (library binding) | ISBN 9781338677133 (ebook)
Subjects: LCSH: Hedgehogs—Juvenile fiction. | Swimming—Juvenile fiction. | Best friends—Juvenile fiction. | CYAC: Hedgehogs—Fiction. | Swimming—Fiction. | Best friends—Fiction. | Friendship—Fiction.
Classification: LCC PZ7.1.F52 Ld 2021 | DDC [E]—dc23
LC record available at https://lccn.loc.gov/2020030126

10 9 8 7 6 5 4 3 2 1   21 22 23 24 25

Printed in China   62
First edition, May 2021
Edited by Katie Carella
Book design by Maria Mercado

3

4

6

7

9

I did forget **one** thing.

Haha!

7

23

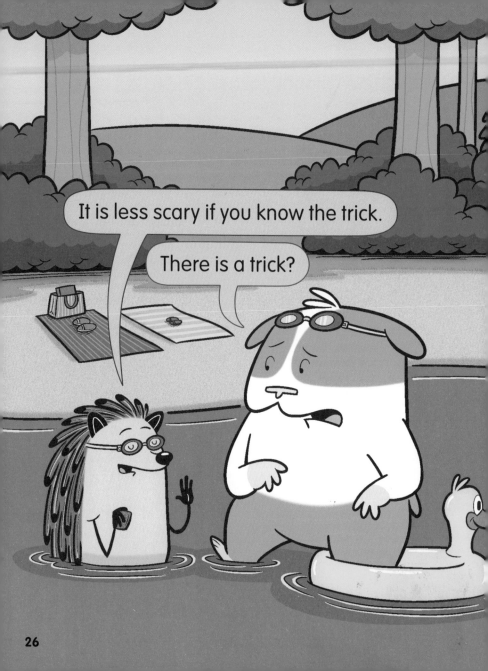

28

29

35

37

43

About the Author

Norm Feuti lives in Massachusetts with his family, a dog, two cats, and a guinea pig. He is the creator of the newspaper comic strips **Retail** and **Gil**. He is also the author and illustrator of the graphic novel **The King of Kazoo**. **Hello, Hedgehog!** is Norm's first early reader series.

YOU CAN DRAW HARRY!

1. Draw a potato shape.

2. Draw the ears, hair, and two big bumps for the mouth!

3. Add legs, feet, and a tail. Give Harry a chin.

4. Draw a tube around his belly, and add two circles on his head for the goggles.

5. Give Harry arms, eyes, and a wide letter T for the nose. Then, give the ducky a beak, hair, and eyes.

6. Color in your drawing!

WHAT'S YOUR STORY?

Harry and Hedgehog like to play water games.
Imagine **you** play Dive for Treasure with them.
What treasures would each of you find?
What other games would you play?
Write and draw your story!

Also by Michael McGarrity

Tularosa

Mexican Hat

Serpent Gate

Hermit's Peak

The Judas Judge

Under the Color of Law

THE BIG GAMBLE